Disney
Fairies

Layouts by Art Mawhinney
Art by the Disney Storybook Artists

Published by
Louis Weber, C.E.O., Publications International, Ltd.
7373 North Cicero Avenue, Lincolnwood, Illinois 60712

Ground Floor, 59 Gloucester Place, London W1U 8JJ

Customer Service: 1-800-595-8484 or customer_service@pilbooks.com

www.pilbooks.com

p i kids is a registered trademark of Publications International, Ltd.

Look and Find is a registered trademark of Publications International, Ltd.,
in the United States and in Canada.

8 7 6 5 4 3 2 1

ISBN-13: 978-1-4127-6479-7
ISBN-10: 1-4127-6479-3

publications international, ltd.

Pixie Hollow, the home of the Never fairies, is nestled in the magical island of Never Land. Today the fairies are busy preparing the Home Tree for the arrival of a new fairy. Can you find these things they have made for her?

Daisy-stem bed

Snack

Spiderweb bedspread

Bouquet of flowers

Cup of lemongrass tea

Violet-petal dress

Faux-mouse slippers

The new fairy, Prilla, has arrived!
Every Never fairy has a special talent,
but Prilla's not sure what hers is yet.
Can you find these fairies—and one
sparrow man—who are among the
best at their talents?

Fira

Bess

Lily

Tink

Beck

Rani

Terence

In the kitchen, Dulcie shows Prilla the ingredients that kitchen talents use. The spices tickle Prilla's nose, making her sneeze. As Prilla snacks on Dulcie's poppy-puff rolls, look for these creations that probably won't make the cut.

Sticky sap sandwich

Pine-needle stew

Pollen cookie

Toadstool casserole

Mud pie

Pumpkin upside-down cake

Walnut-shell crunch cake

Prilla visits Tinker Bell's workshop. Tink hopes that Prilla will be a pots-and-pans talent like she is, but Prilla's talent lies elsewhere. As Prilla continues the search for her calling, look for these troubled pots and pans.

Loopy ladle

Dented dew pot

Clogged colander

Collapsed cooling rack

Missing-muffin tin

Beat-up brownie pan

Fractured frying pan

Prilla has wandered into Lily's beautiful garden, where the Cuddle Vine has taken a fancy to her. While she frees herself from its embrace, look for these colorful flowers and accessories.

This Ever tree fruit

This lilac

Lily's umbrella

Iris's leafkerchief

This snapdragon

This wild rose

This poppy

Rani shows Prilla Havendish Stream, where Prilla has lots of questions for the swimming fairy. While Rani tries to answer them, see if you can spot these amazing things in and around the water.

This dragonfly

This shell

This wishing fountain

This tree frog

This hummingbird

This baby turtle

This water lily

Beck is trying to teach Prilla a few words in Chipmunk, but it's not an easy language to learn. Luckily, some of the chipmunks are pretty chatty—especially these. Can you find them?

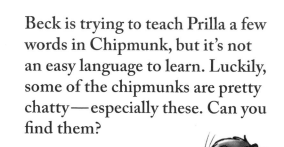

Prilla wishes she were a light-talent fairy like Fira and Luna. "Every creature is special," Queen Clarion tells her. "Soon you will understand your talent." Each creature *is* special! See if you can find these unique fireflies.

Flitter back to the Home Tree and find the hearts that these talent groups are creating to make Prilla feel welcome.

Sewing talent

Garden talent

Pots-and-pans talent

Water talent

Baking talent

Light talent

Fly back to the courtyard and see if you can find these other special fairies (and one sparrow man).

Dulcie

Fawn

Aidan

Silvermist

Vidia

Rosetta

Follow your nose back to the Home Tree kitchen and look for these fairy delicacies.

Acorn soufflé

Ever tree fruit preserves

Bluebell soup

Fresh fern salad

Dew

Crustless tea sandwich

Green-grass tea

Work your way back to Tinker Bell's workshop and try to spot these tools of her trade.

Tinker's hammer

Spool of metal wire

Scissors

Steel-wool lamb

Pliers

Ruler

Amble back to Lily's garden and try to find these creatures that help it grow.

Bumblebee

This butterfly

Ladybug

Caterpillar

Earthworm

Spider

Where there is water, there are rainbows! Dive back into Havendish Stream and see if you can find seven rainbows there.

Can you talk to animals? Scurry back to the Never forest and have a chat with these woodland creatures.

Bluebird

Hedgehog

Twitter

Nan

Squirrel

Grandfather Mole

Raccoon

Flutter back to the nighttime firefly performance and find these other things that shine.

Lamp

Constellation

Torch

Moon

Candle

Lantern